BABY'S BRIS

Susan Wilkowski
illustrated by Judith Friedman

KAR-BEN COPIES INC. ROCKVILLE, MD

For Mario,
with admiration, gratitude, and deep love
— SW

Library of Congress Cataloging-in-Publication Data

Wilkowski, Susan.
Baby's Bris / Susan Wilkowski : illustrated by Judith Friedman.
p. cm.
Summary: Sophie becomes a big sister and, during the first eight days of her brother's life, learns about the custom of bris (circumcision) and celebrates the event with her family and new brother Ben.
ISBN 1-58013-052-6 (hc.) — ISBN 1-58013-053-4 (pbk.)
[1. Circumcision — Religious aspects — Judaism Fiction. 2. Judaism — Customs and practices Fiction. 3. Babies — Fiction. 4. Brother and sisters — Fiction.] I. Friedman, Judith, 1945- ill.
II. Title.
PZ7.W65435Bab 1999
[Fic] — dc 21

99-24803
CIP

Published by Kar-Ben Copies, Inc. Rockville, MD 1-800-4KARBEN
Printed in Mexico

The day Sophie became a big sister, Auntie Luba held her close and gushed, "Mazel tov. You have a baby brother. So lucky you are!"

Sophie squirmed from Auntie's arms and watched her dab tears that trickled from her eyes.

"Why are you crying?" Sophie asked.

"These are happy tears," Luba began. "I cry because I'm happy. And I cry because today is so special for you."

Sophie never heard of happy tears. And she wondered why this day was so special for *her.* Still, she hoped a day so special meant double-fudge cookies for dessert and staying up extra late.

She found, instead, that it meant a bell that chimed and chimed.

A phone that rang and rang.

And an aunt that talked and talked.

"Rebecca had the baby," Auntie Luba would say... "a boy...the bris will be next Tuesday...Mazel tov to you, too."

The second day Sophie was a big sister, she visited Mama in the hospital.

"My big girl," Mama said, hugging her tight. "Come see our new baby."

They walked down the hall to the nursery. Sophie looked through the big window at the tiny babies.

"Over there," Daddy pointed. "In the corner. That's your brother, Sophie." He and Mama leaned so close, they fogged the glass.

Sophie stayed put.

The third day Sophie was a big sister, Baby came home. He was wrapped in a soft blanket. Just his face peeked out.

"Look at his eyes," Auntie Luba said, cradling him gently. "He has Papa Benny's eyes. He'll see the world through Papa's smiling eyes."

Sophie went to the wall where the family pictures hung. She looked closely at Papa Benny. His eyes were dark blue, almost purple. She didn't think his eyes matched Baby's. But standing so close to his picture made Sophie remember the silly songs Papa Benny used to sing to her.

The fourth day Sophie was a big sister, Grandpa and Nana came with their big brown suitcase and bags and bags of Nana's tasty foods.

"Sophie, Sweet Sophie!" Grandpa called, his arms open wide. Sophie flew into them.

"So big you got, Sweet Sophie. So big," he said.

Sophie reached into Grandpa's shirt pocket. He always hid treats there. Usually a stick of licorice, sometimes a colorful shell. This time she found a small shiny box. In the box was a gold star on a chain.

"You're a big sister now," Grandpa explained. "That's an important thing to be, a big sister. So this gift is an important gift."

Sophie thought Grandpa was making too much of this big sister business. Still, she let Nana help her put on her new necklace. And Sophie helped Nana load the freezer with her special foods.

"No one makes rugelach like your Nana's rugelach," Nana declared.

That night after a big Shabbat dinner, friends and neighbors came by to nosh and chat and celebrate Baby.

Sophie celebrated Nana's rugelach.

The fifth day Sophie was a big sister, she went with Daddy and Nana and Grandpa to the synagogue.

"Mazel tov!" said Rabbi Wohlberg. "I look forward to the bris."

"Mazel tov!" said Mr. and Mrs. Weinstein. "We'll bring a little schnapps to the bris."

"Mazel tov!" said Mrs. Greene. "I'll make a nice whitefish salad for the bris."

"Bris, bris, bris," Sophie cried. "Was everyone as excited when I had *my* bris?"

Nana sighed, and drew Sophie near. "When you were born, sweet Sophie, we were filled with such love and joy that it felt like the sun was shining just for us. And we celebrated your birth in a very special way."

Sophie listened carefully.

"It wasn't a bris," Nana continued, "because those are just for boys. Your ceremony was called a Simchat Bat. We danced and sang and thanked God for blessing us with you, our beautiful Sophie. And," Nana added, "Mrs. Greene made a nice whitefish salad for your party, too."

The sixth day Sophie was a big sister, kissing cousins Shelly and Stanley came. They kissed Sophie and Auntie Luba and Mama and Daddy and Nana and Grandpa. And they kissed Baby's fingers and toes and took a good, long look at him. "He seems wise," Shelly said. "He has a wise way about him."

"Yes," said Stanley. "Maybe he'll be wise like Great Uncle Saul was."

Sophie never knew Great Uncle Saul, so Luba touched his picture. "This man," she said. "This is Great Uncle Saul. He was a knowing man, a smart man." Sophie studied the picture. He did look smart, she thought. Then she looked at Baby.

He looked sleepy.

The seventh day Sophie was a big sister, Auntie Luba took her shopping.

"For the bris," Luba said, "you should have a new dress."

"I can get a new dress?" Sophie asked. "Even if the bris isn't for me?"

"The bris is not just for Baby." Auntie Luba stroked Sophie's hair. "It's for you, too. It's for all of us."

Sophie didn't think Baby's bris was for anyone but Baby, but she had fun picking out a flowery dress with a big bow.

"Now Baby needs something special to wear," Luba said. They walked up the block to a small shop. Auntie Luba told the storekeeper about the new baby. "He needs his first kippah," she said.

"I wish you a hearty Mazel tov!" the man replied. He placed a basket of tiny yarmulkes on the glass counter.

"You pick, Sophie," Auntie said.

Sophie looked carefully at each of them. Then she smiled and picked one up. "I like the color in this one," she said. "Dark blue, almost purple."

The eighth day Sophie was a big sister, she went to her baby brother's bris.

The house filled early with friends and relatives and good food and drink. Baby was upstairs with Mama. When the mohel arrived, everyone gathered in the living room. It was time.

Kissing cousins Shelly and Stanley carried Baby into the room on a big, lacy pillow. Daddy proudly took his son and set him on Grandpa's lap.

"With the birth of each child," the mohel began, "we make a promise." He held Baby high for everyone to see. "Today, each of us, in our own way, promises to help this baby grow to be a good Jewish man. A man who knows God's laws and does good deeds. This ceremony is a symbol of our promise."

Sophie slipped her hand into Luba's. "Is it my promise, too?" she asked.

"It's yours too, Sophie. It's very much yours." Luba pointed to the wall of pictures and added, "It was theirs, too."

"They promised?" Sophie asked.

"They did. Everyone who came before and everyone who is yet to come. Everyone promises. Everyone's linked." Sophie ran her fingers along her new chain. She felt how each tiny circle was connected to the one before. And to the next.

“Blessed are You, O God, who has given us the mitzvah of this bris,” the mohel sang, placing Baby back on Grandpa’s lap. He opened Baby’s diaper and removed a small bit of skin from him. Baby cried, but stopped as soon as he was warm in his blanket again.

“Is Baby okay?” Sophie asked Luba.

“He’s fine, Sophie. He’s just fine.”

Daddy and Mama recited a second blessing to welcome Baby to the Jewish people.

"Mazel tov!" everyone cheered. "Mazel tov!"

The mohel sang kiddush over a cup of wine. Then the room became perfectly still as he looked toward Mama and Daddy to reveal Baby's name.

"This is Benjamin Saul," Daddy called out. "May he live a life full of laughter and love, like our Papa Benny."

"And be eager to learn and grow wise like our Great Uncle Saul," Mama added.

"May we all come together again to celebrate his Bar Mitzvah," Stanley joined in.

"And again to see him standing under his wedding chuppah," Shelly said.

Grandpa rose from his seat, Benny snug in his arms. "Benjamin Saul should one day know the joy of passing on our traditions to a child of his own."

Daddy cried tears Sophie knew were happy ones.

"Let's celebrate Benny as we welcome him into our Jewish family," Mama announced.

Everyone feasted and sang and drank and couldn't get over how delicious Nana's rugelach were.

But Sophie had something more important to do.

She had a promise to keep.

"Can I hold Benny?" she asked Mama.

"Of course you can," Mama said.

Sophie sat on the couch near the wall of family pictures. She held Benny close. "You have to try to be good," she whispered, letting his tiny hand squeeze her finger.

"There is so much I need to teach you about," she said, feeling big and smart. "Like Grandpa," she went on. "He hides treats in his shirt pocket. And Nana," Sophie said, smiling, "makes the best rugelach." Then she looked deep into Benny's eyes.

"And Papa Benny. He used to sing the silliest songs to me. Do you want to hear one?"

Sophie made a funny face and sang a silly song.

Just for Benny.

On the day of his bris.

ABOUT THE BRIS

Brit Milah (colloquially called a *bris*) means Covenant of Circumcision. The ceremony, held on the 8th day of a Jewish baby boy's life, is a sign of the covenant between God and the Jewish people. As a symbolic act, a minor operation is performed in which the foreskin of the baby's penis is removed.

The bris is usually performed by a *mohel*, a person trained in both Jewish ritual and in the procedure of circumcision. Some families choose to have a doctor perform the brit milah and a rabbi or cantor recite the ritual blessings.

Traditionally, the ceremony is held at home, though it may be held in a hospital or synagogue. Two people, selected to be the baby's godfather and godmother (*kvater and kvaterin* in Yiddish), bring the baby into the room. The baby may wear a *kippah* (or *yarmulke*), a ritual skullcap. A relative or close friend (often one of the baby's grandfathers) is chosen as the *sandek,* the person who holds the baby while the circumcision is performed. Some families set aside a ceremonial *Chair for Elijah* for the baby's circumcision. Elijah is the prophet who will announce the coming of the messiah and is a symbolic guest at every Passover seder and bris.

Kiddush, a blessing recited over a cup of wine, is sung to proclaim the holiness of the occasion. It is customary to wait to reveal the baby's name at the bris. Among Eastern European Jews, children are traditionally named for relatives who have died. The parents may choose to give a short talk recalling the people for whom the baby is being named.

A celebratory meal (*seudat mitzvah)* follows the ceremony.

Glossary

Bar Mitzvah — "son of the commandment" — the coming of age ceremony for a 13-year-old Jewish boy

Chuppah — wedding canopy

Covenant — a promise or pact

Mazel tov! — "Good luck!" — words of congratulations

Mitzvah — commandment

Rugelach — cookies filled with nuts and raisins — a traditional Jewish dessert

Schnapps — alcoholic drink

Shabbat — the Jewish Sabbath which begins Friday at sundown and lasts until Saturday after sundown

Shalom Zachar — a welcome party for a baby boy held on the Friday night after his birth

Simchat Bat — "rejoicing in a daughter" — a ceremony held to celebrate the birth of a baby girl